Sophie
Star Child

For more information about special discounts for bulk purchases, please contact
Light Technology Publishing Special Sales at 1-800-450-0985 / 928-526-1345 or
publishing@LightTechnology.net.
Also available as an e-book from your favorite e-book distributor.

ISBN-13: 978-1-62233-021-8
Published and printed in the United States of America by:

A DIVISION OF
LIGHT TECHNOLOGY
PUBLISHING

PO Box 3540 • Flagstaff, AZ 86003 • 800-450-0985 • (928) 526-1345
www.LightTechnology.com

Sophie StarChild

WRITTEN BY TRACY ULOMA COOPER

ILLUSTRATED BY ERIC ROGERSON

STARCHILD

PRESS

A DIVISION OF
LIGHT TECHNOLOGY
PUBLISHING

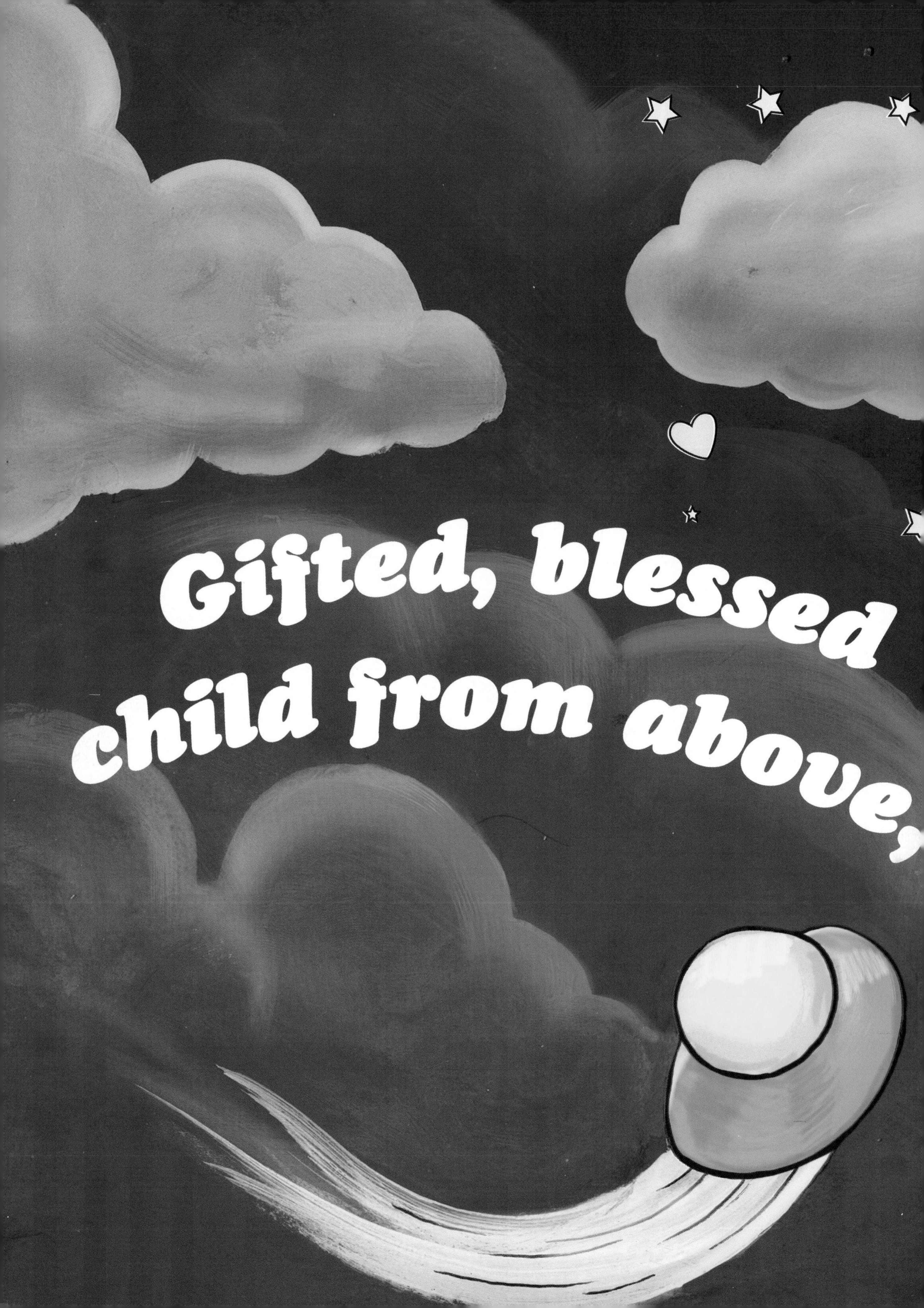

Gifted, blessed child from above,

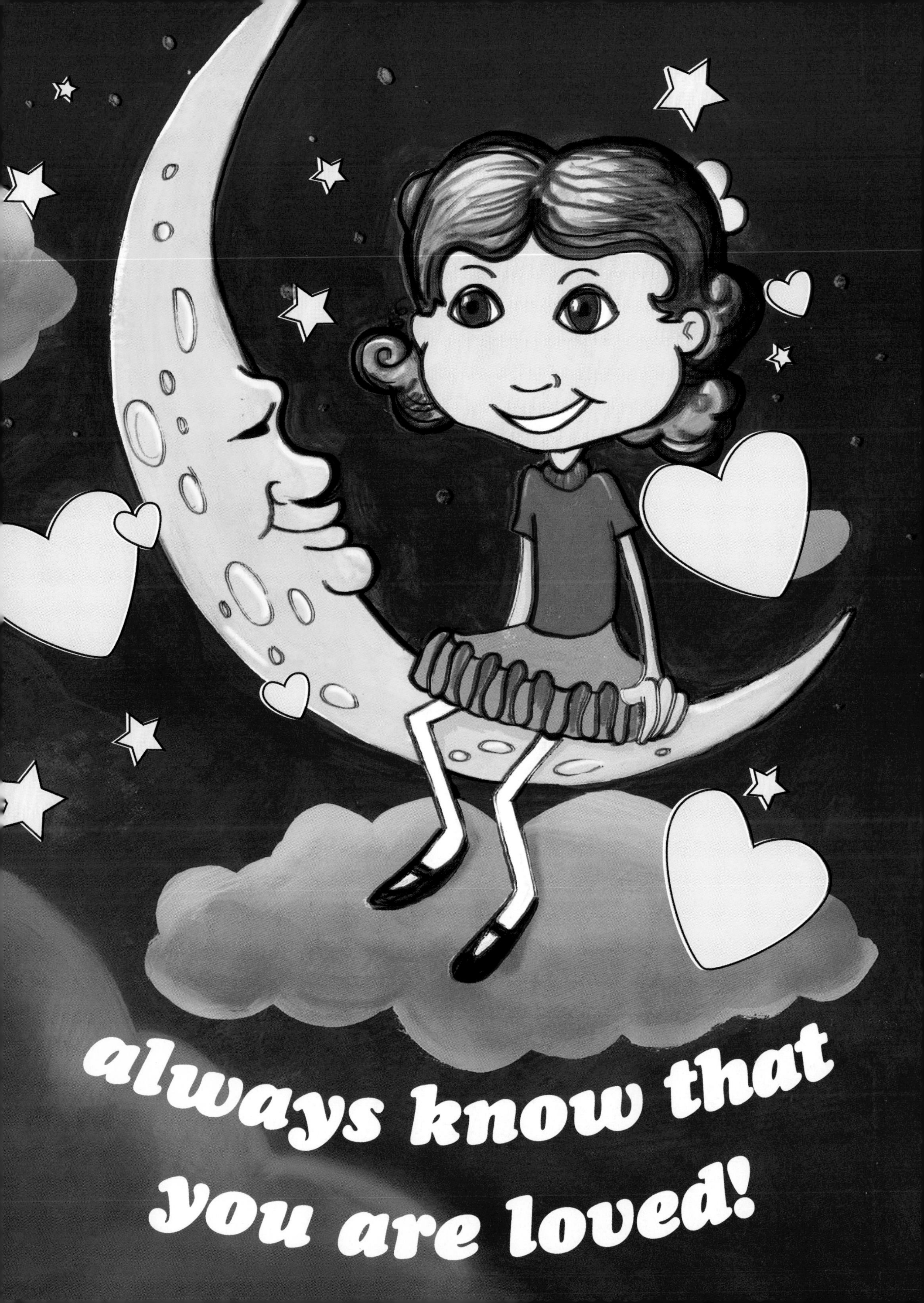

always know that you are loved!

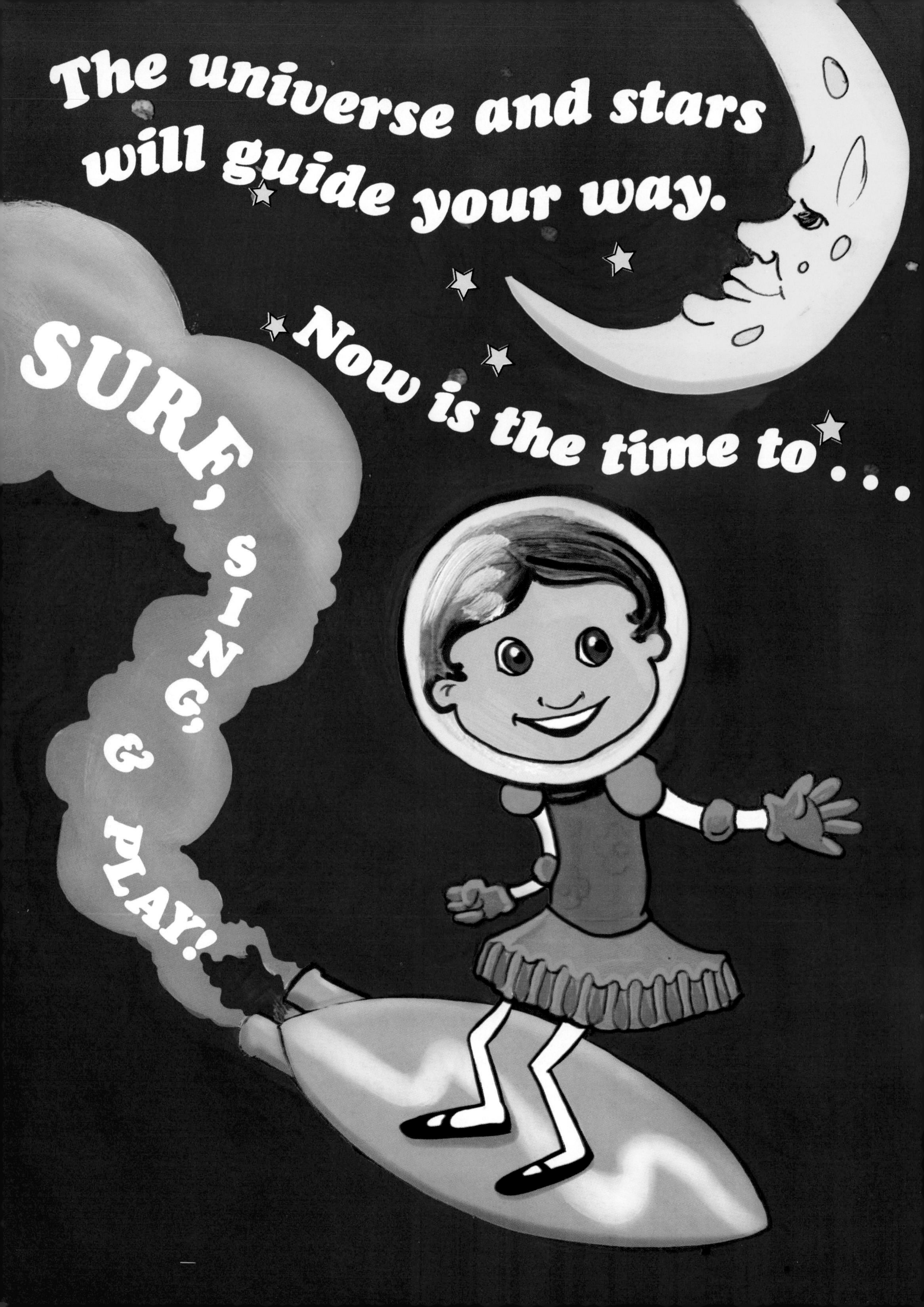
The universe and stars will guide your way.
Now is the time to...
SURF, SING, & PLAY!

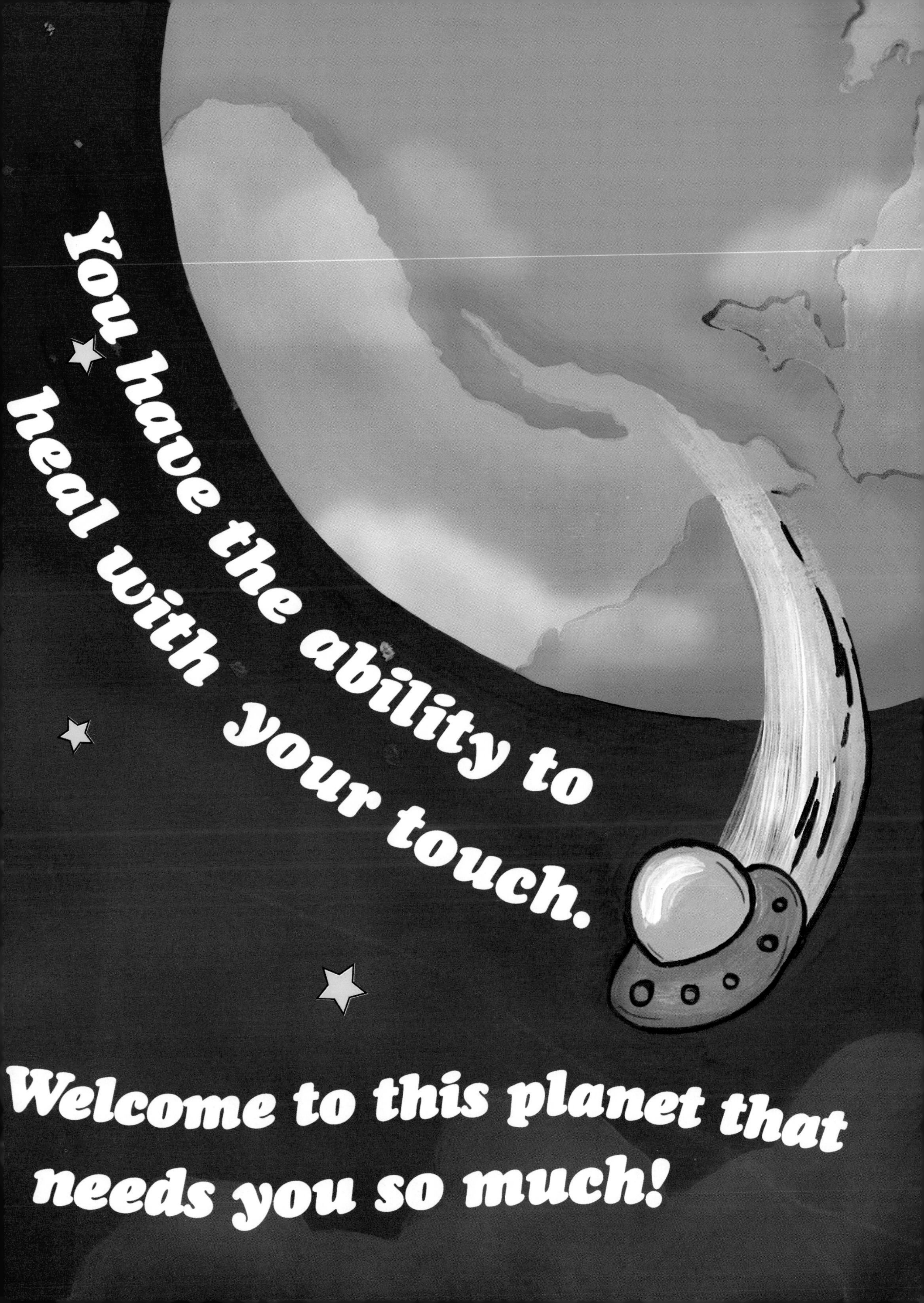

You have the ability to heal with your touch.

Welcome to this planet that needs you so much!

Release
all heaviness,
sadness, and fear.
For YOU...
the answers
will always
appear!

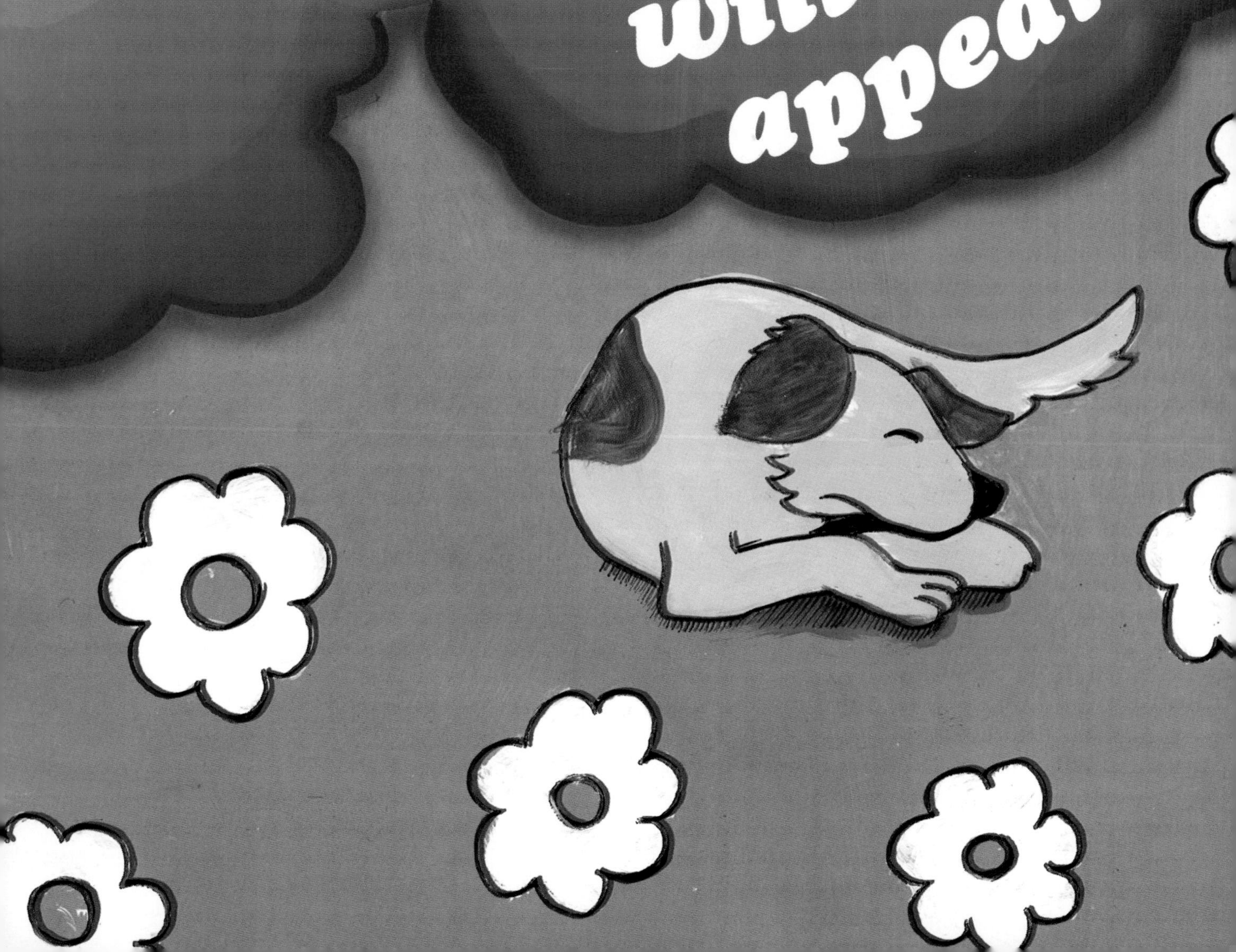

You are protected when
asleep or awake,
at rest or at play,
and from night to
daybreak!

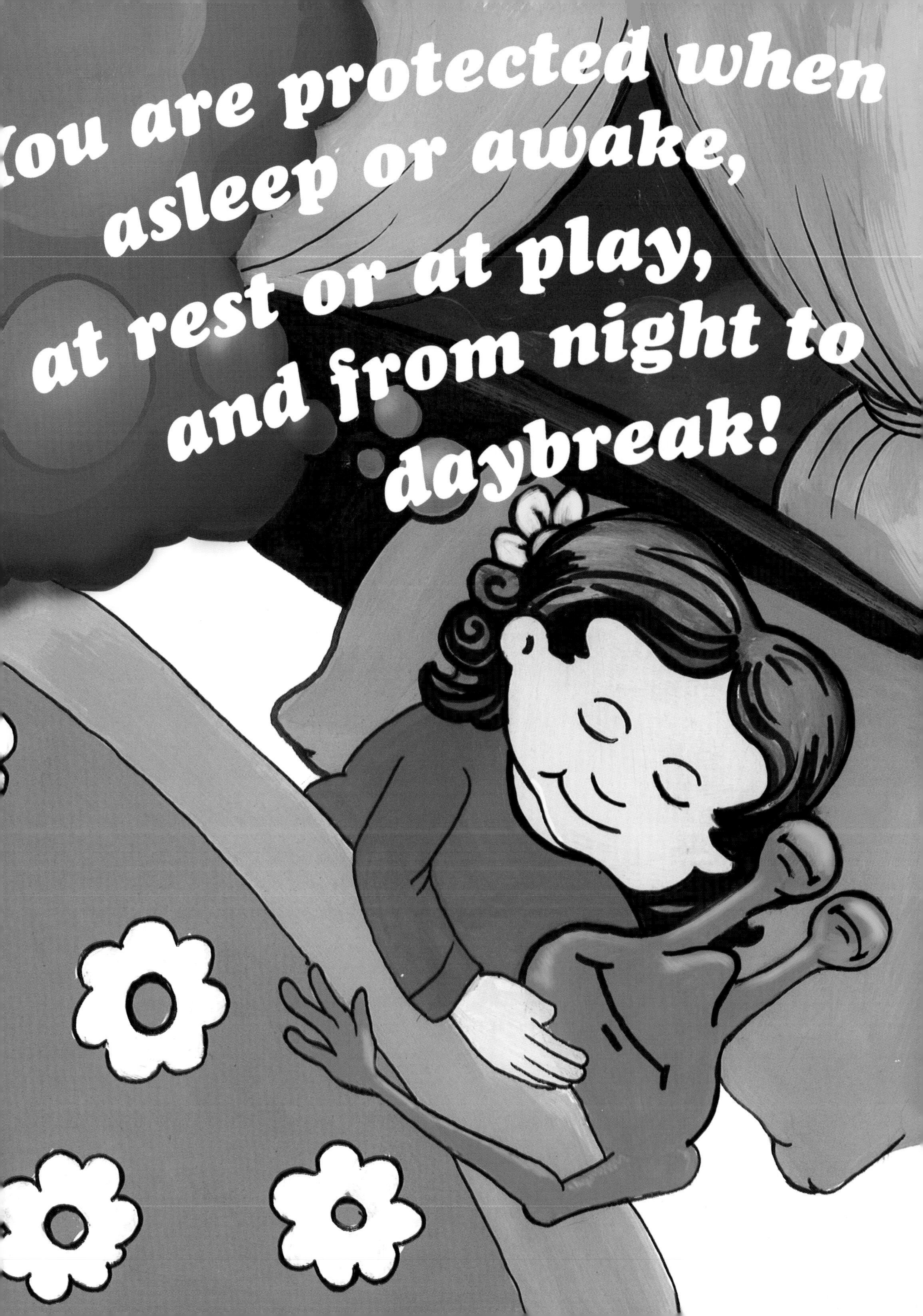

No need to be lost in a sea filled with fears.

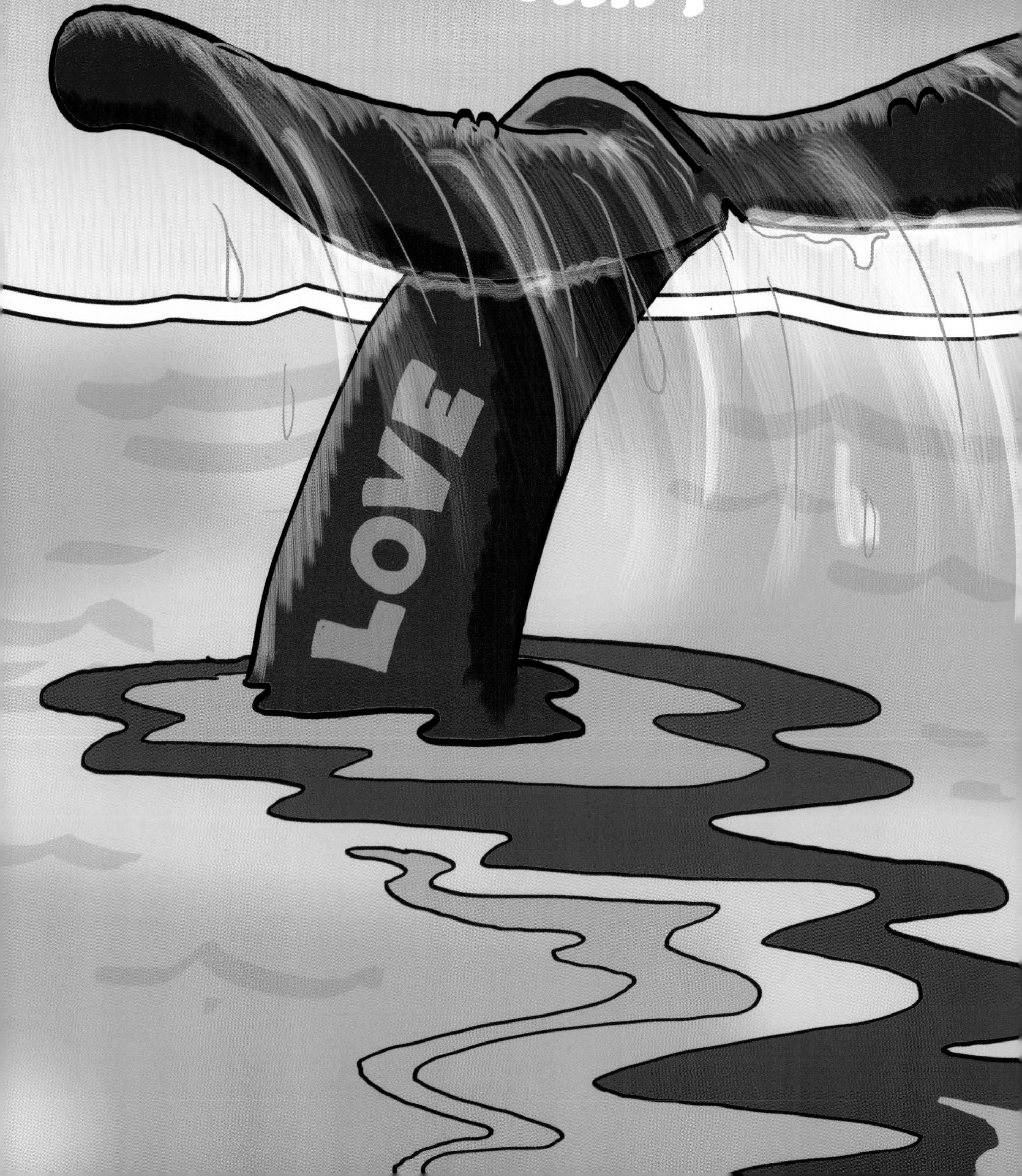
LOVE

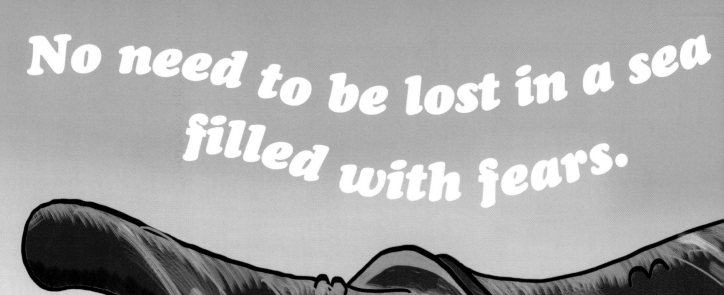

Love is much stronger than what could bring you to tears.

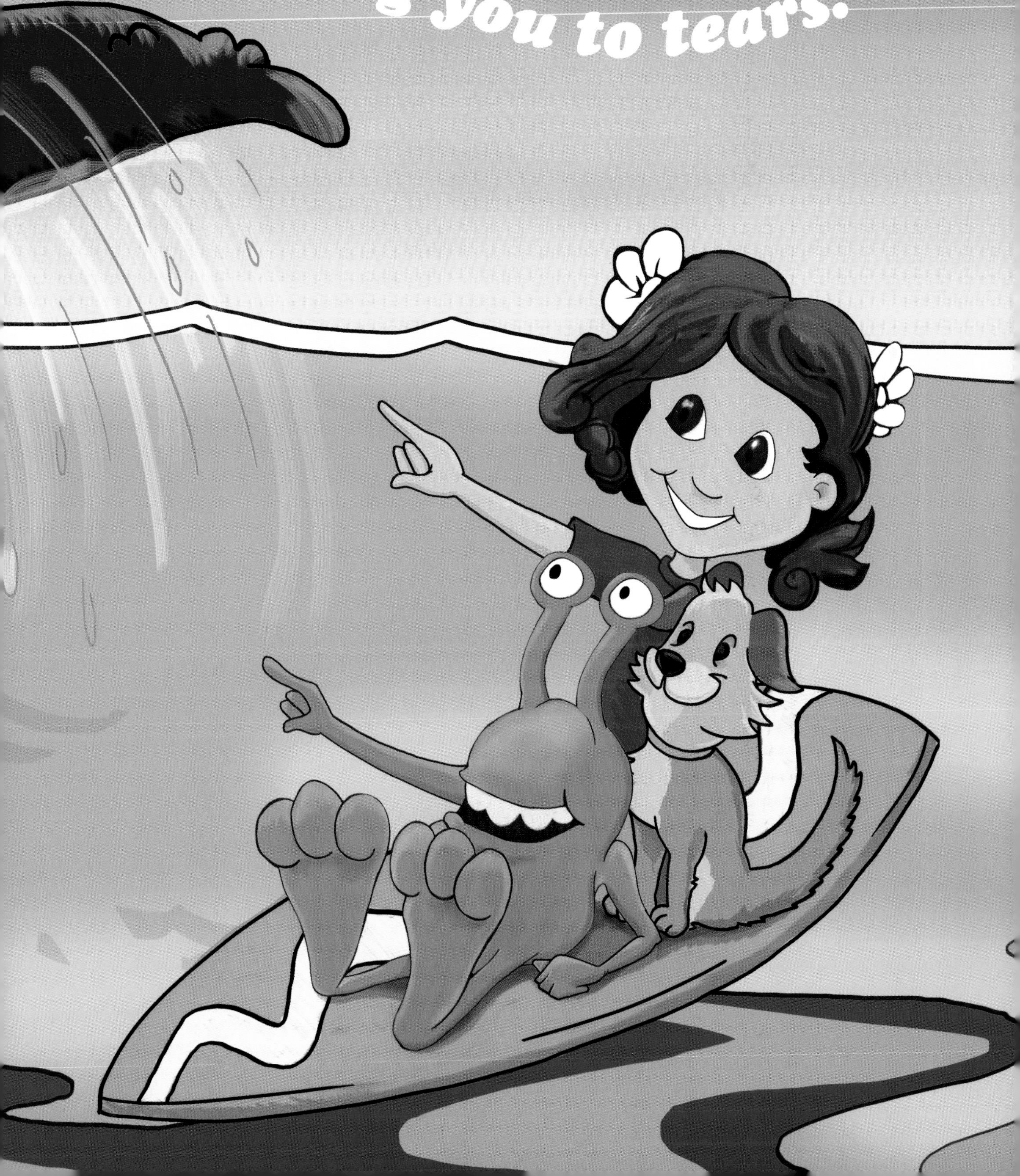

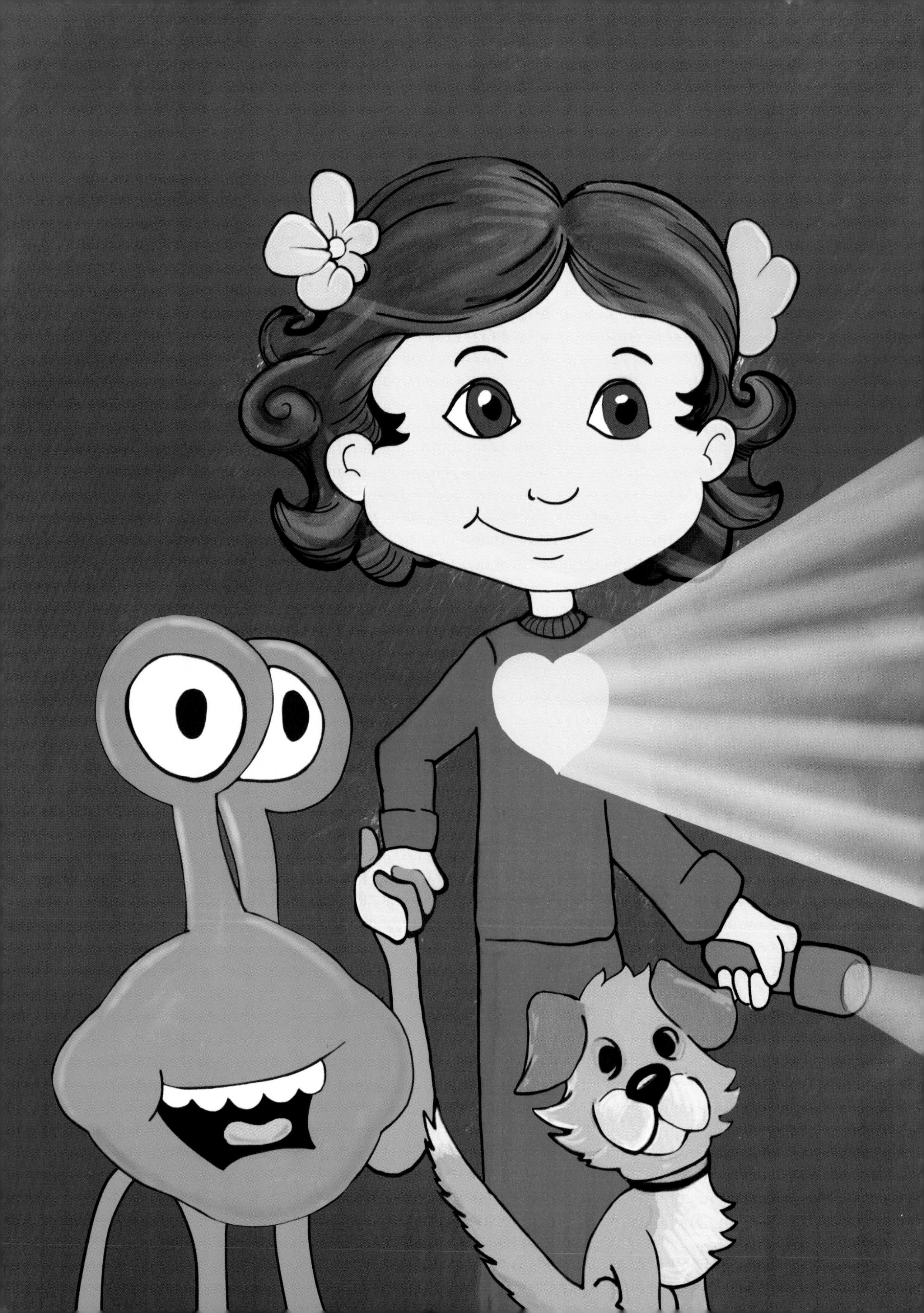

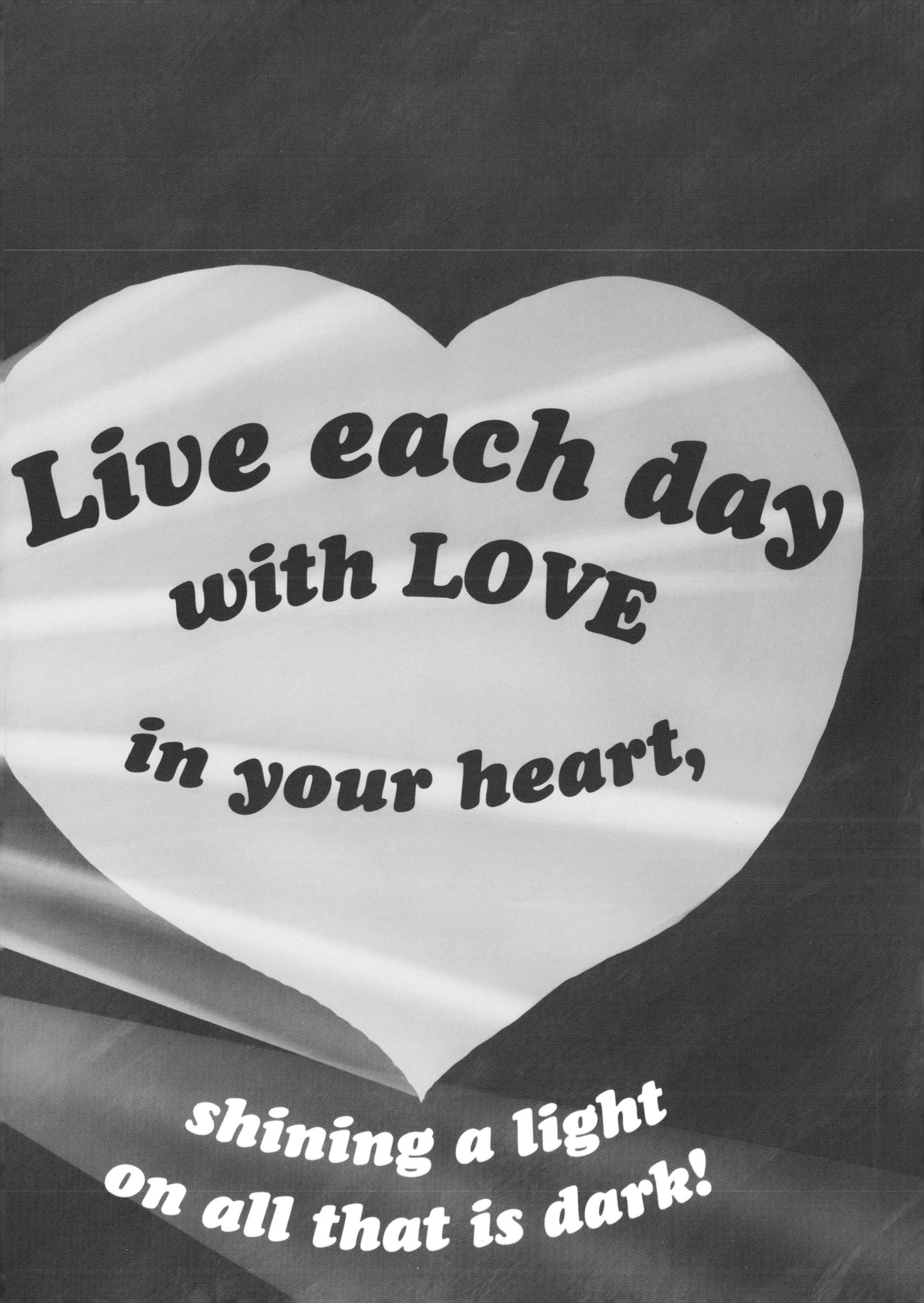
Live each day
with LOVE
in your heart,
shining a light
on all that is dark!

You will help the world
to lift and ascend,
especially with help from
other star children friends

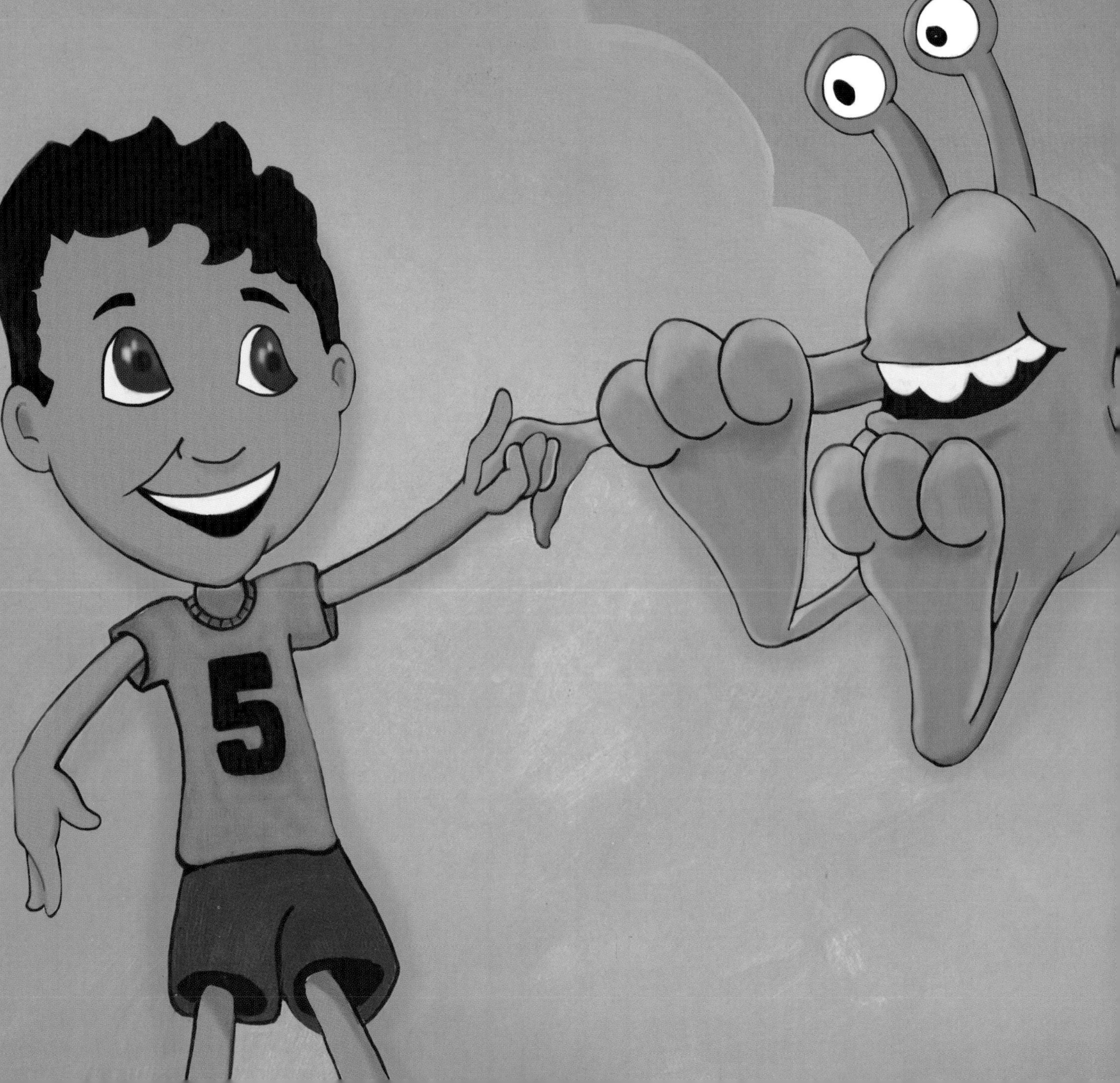

You all hold great truth
and wisdom within.
The spread of love and
peace now may begin!

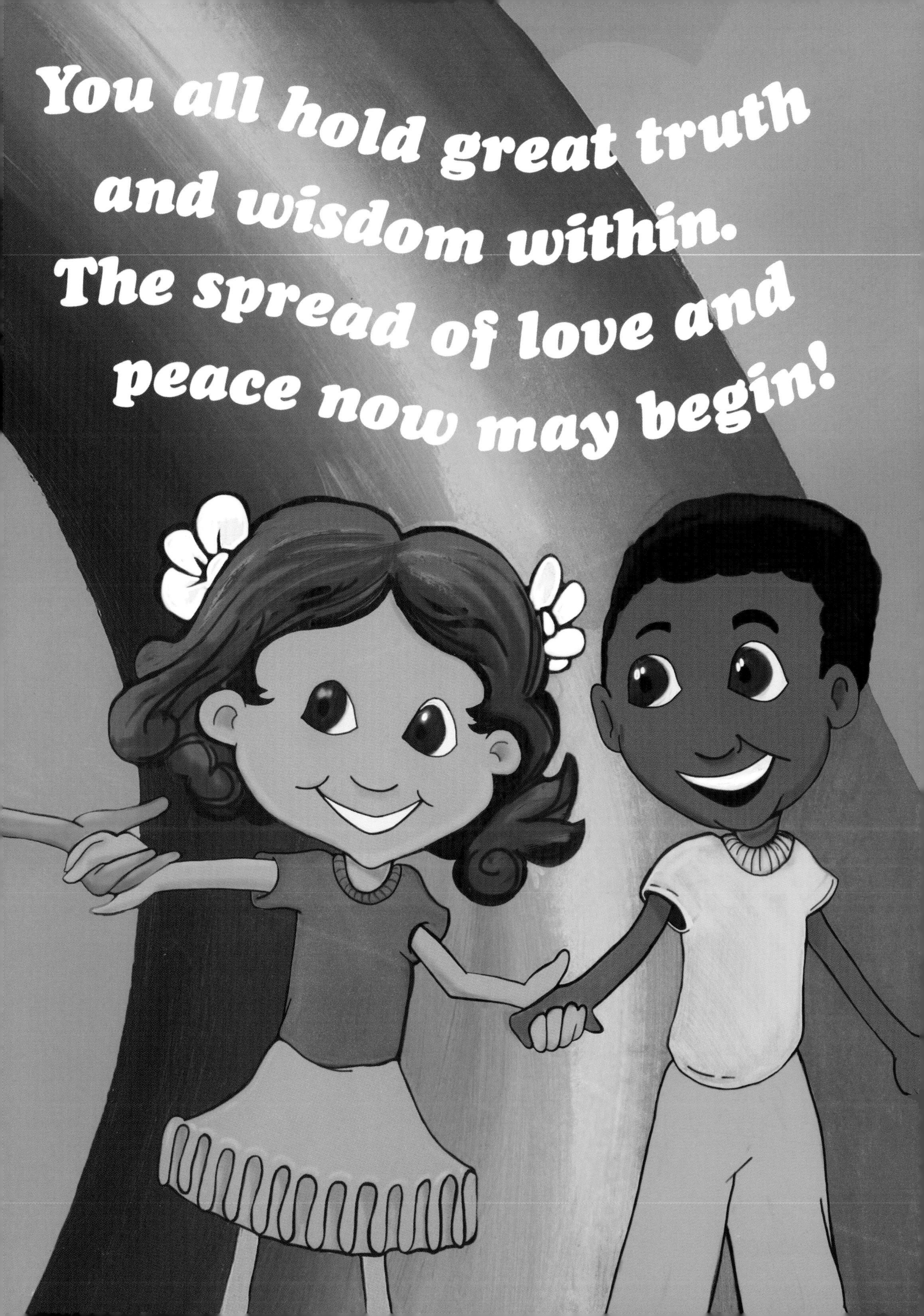

Artists and ambassadors to a better world,

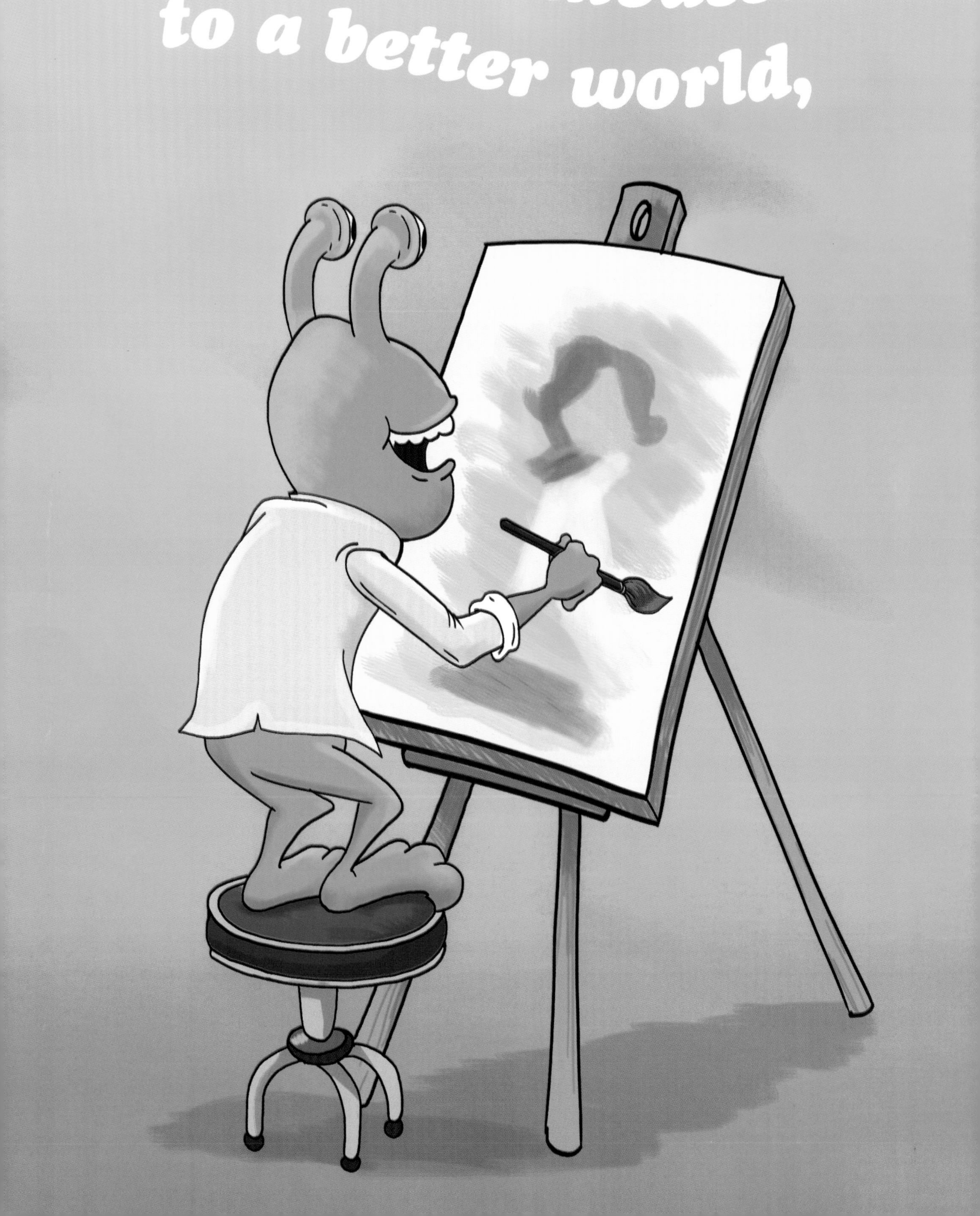

Believe in yourselves to see your powers unfurl!

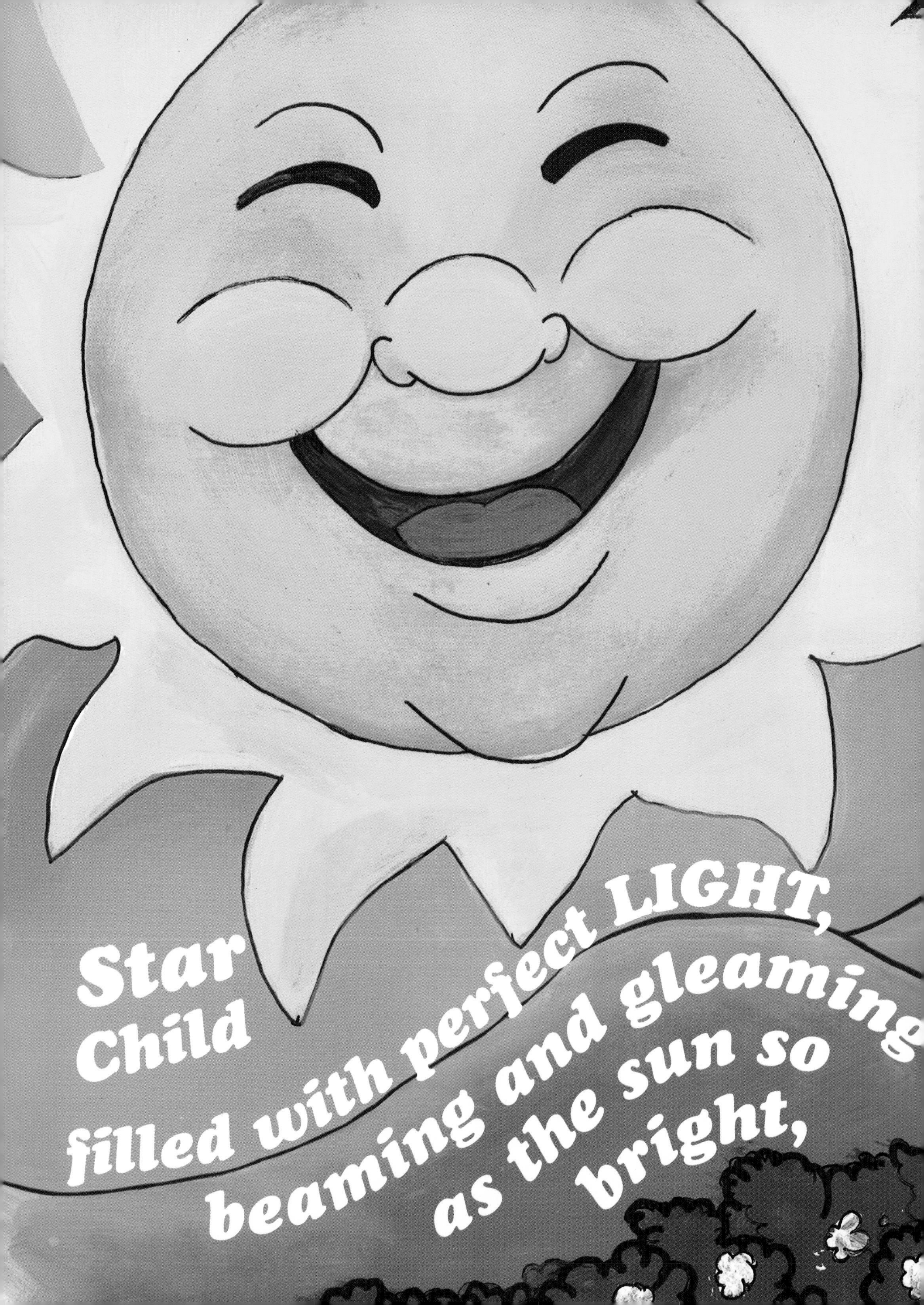

Star Child
filled with perfect LIGHT,
beaming and gleaming
as the sun so bright,

you are dear, child,
special and divine,

peaceful and creative,
absolutely sublime.

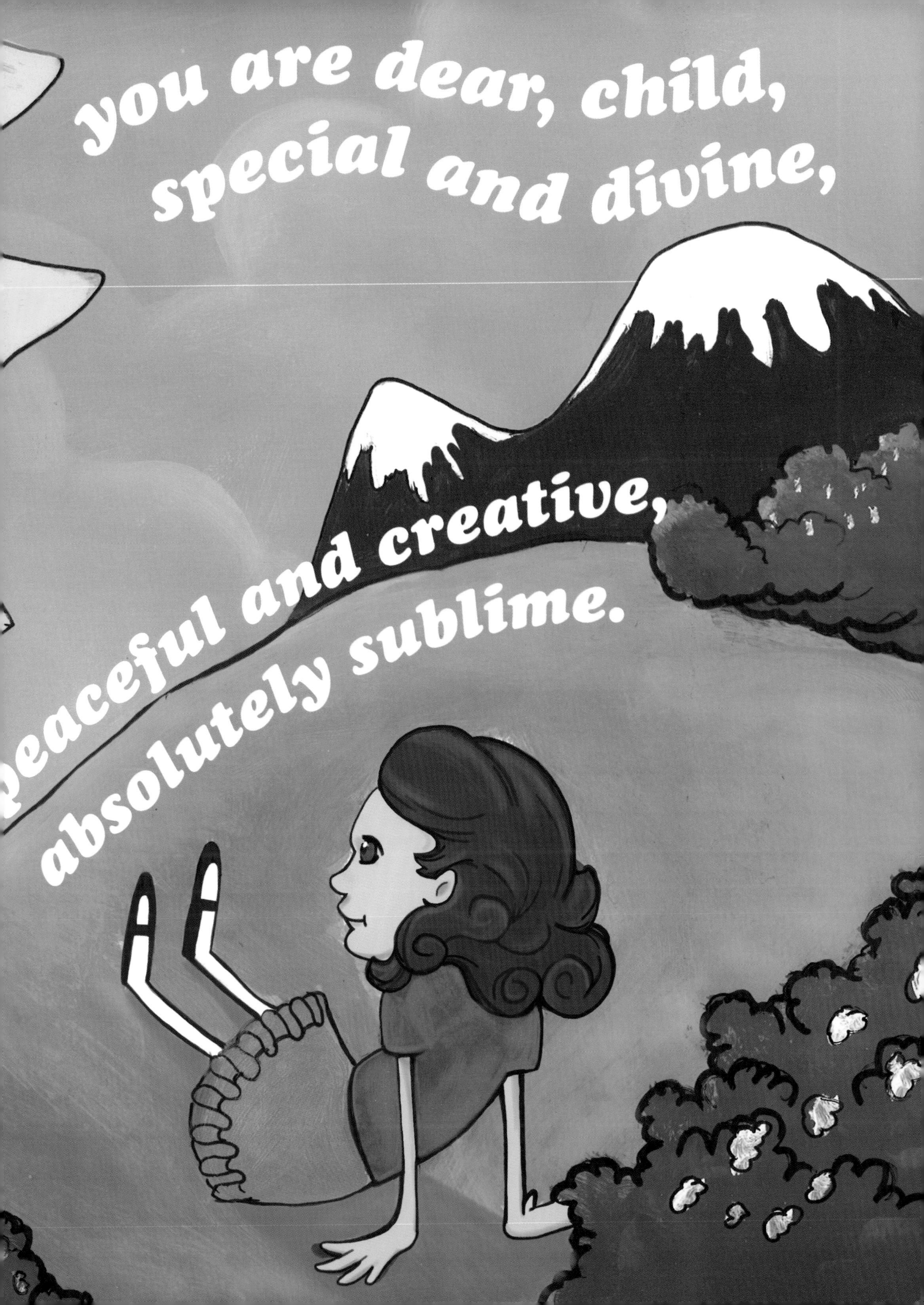

Be a scientist or an engineer,
and design a world
to many a cheer!

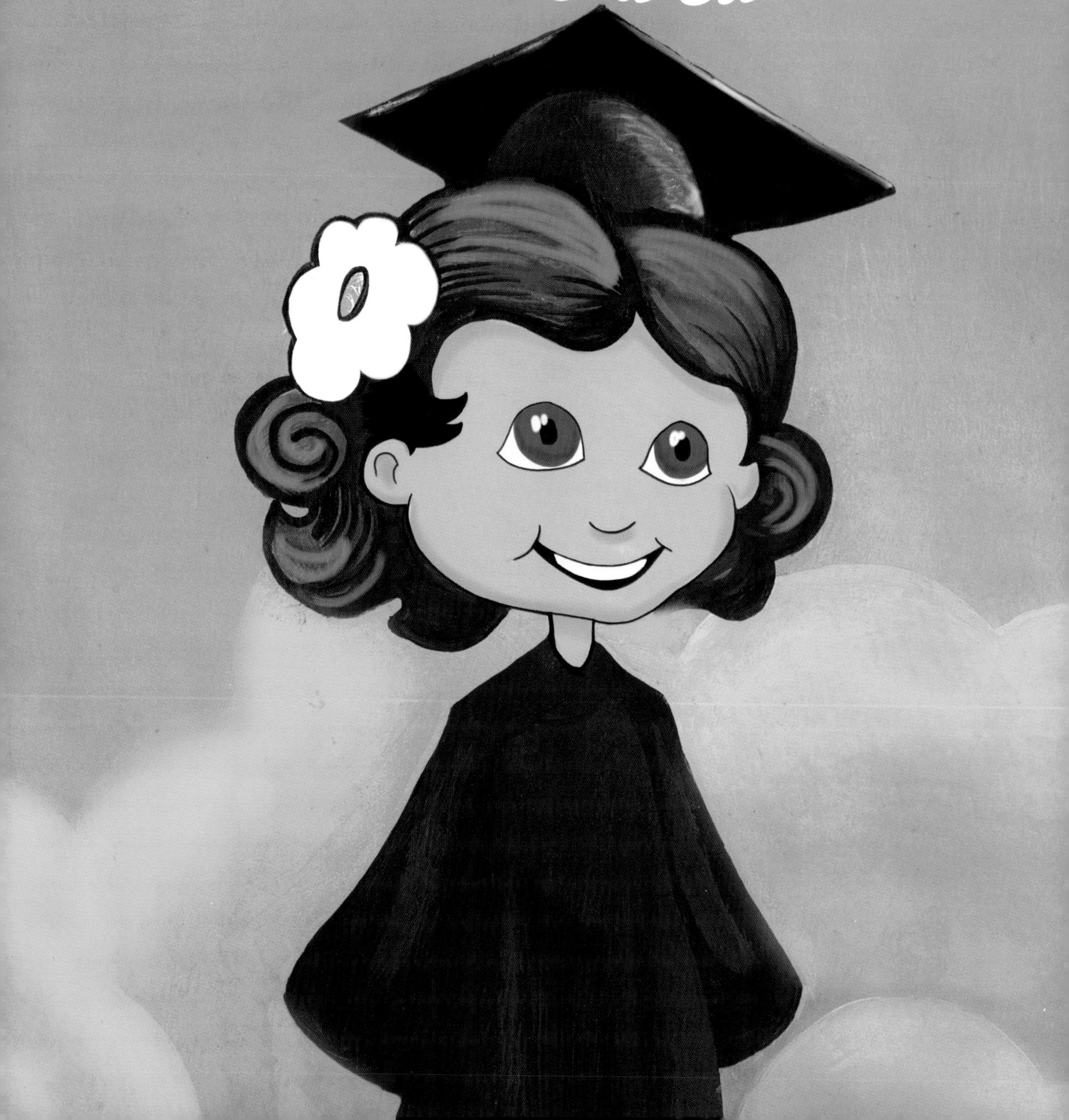

A doctor, a healer -
-whatever you'll be, you'll
make a brighter future
for all to see.

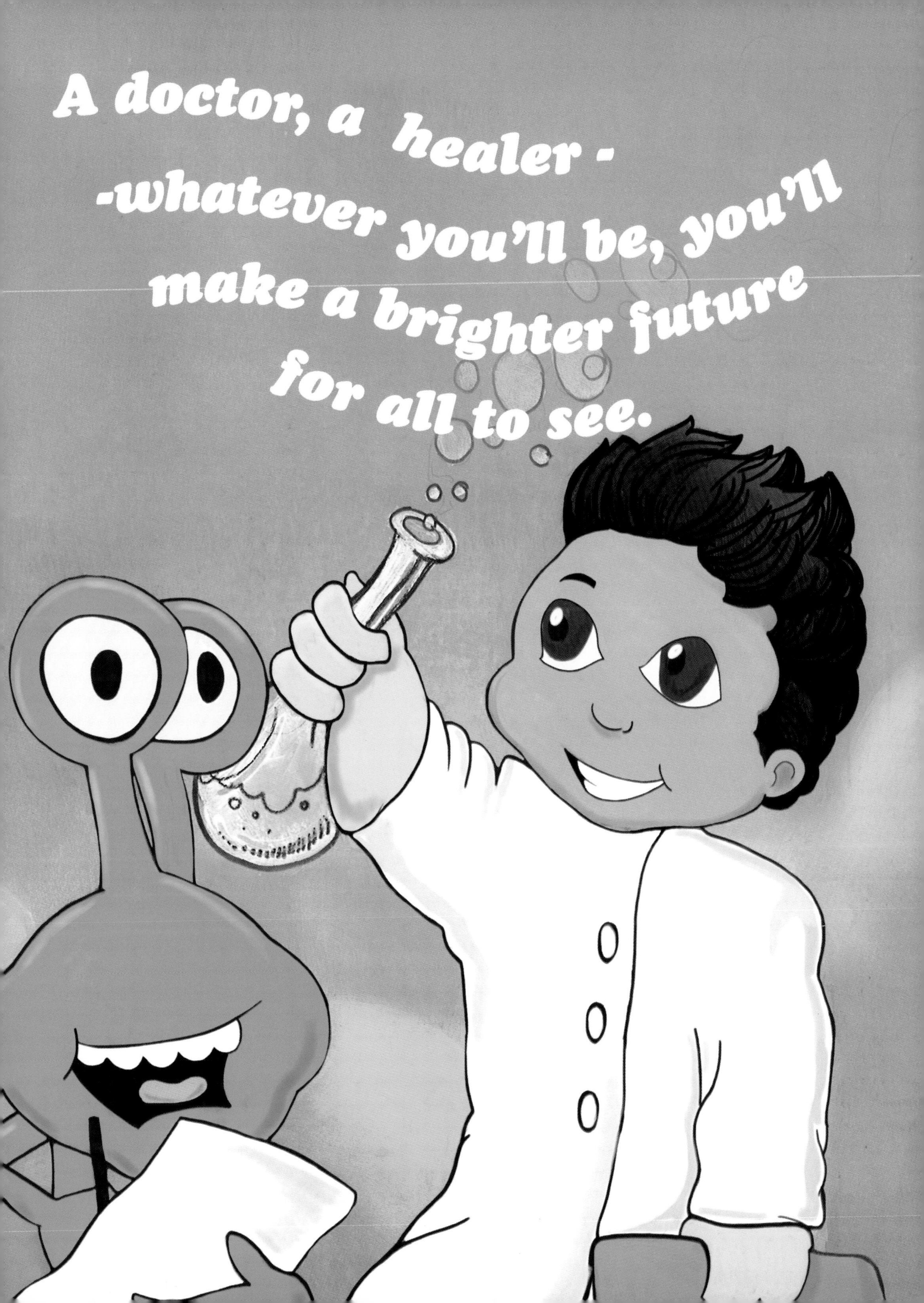

Thank you, thank you for your gifts from above.

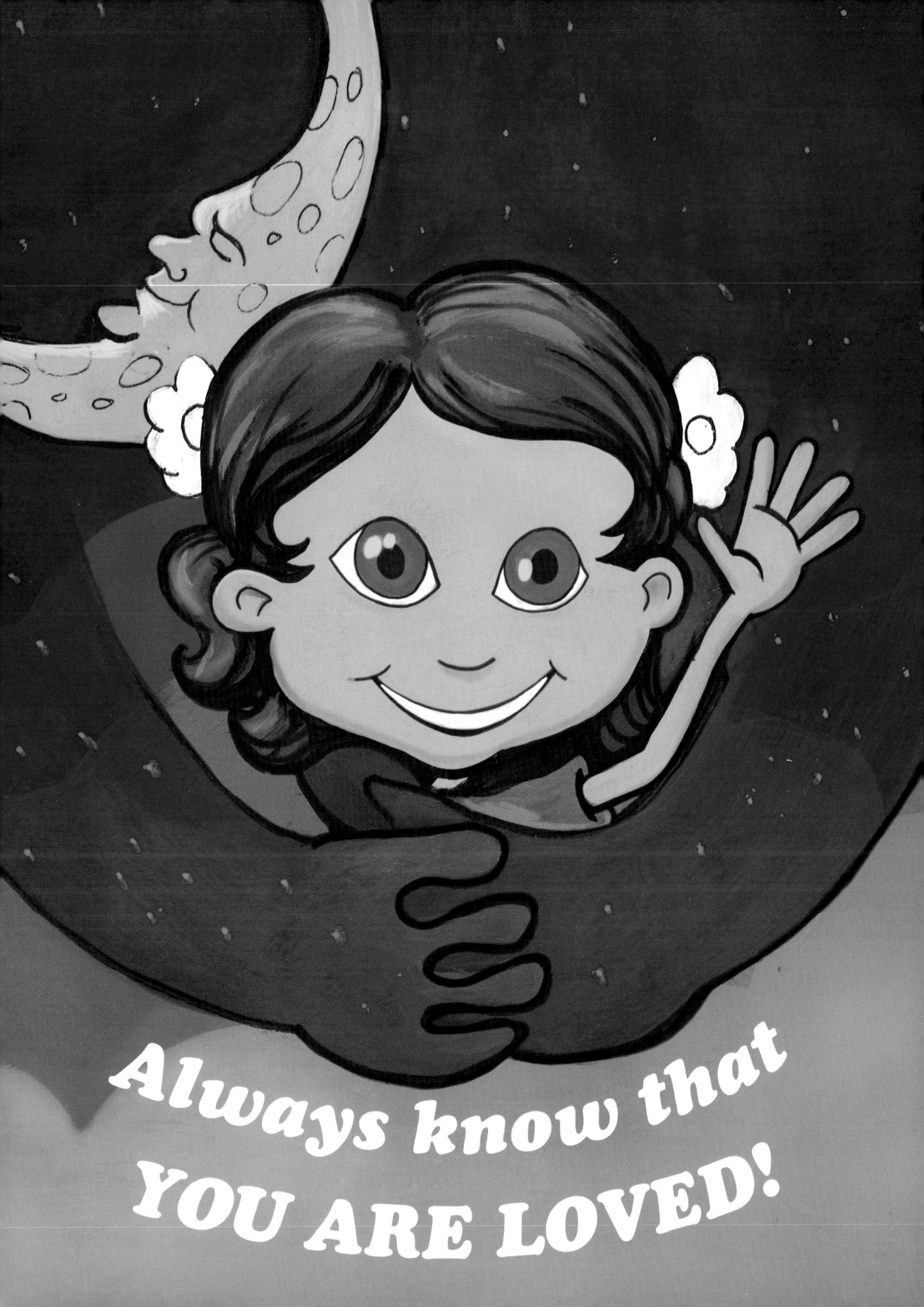

Always know that
YOU ARE LOVED!

Create a picture of what you want to be

CREATIVE COLLABORATORS

Tracy Uloma Cooper, PhD, hails from the Bay Area and was raised under the teachings of Unity and *A Course in Miracles*. Previously with UC Berkeley's Psychological Services department, Tracy now strives to share the message of unconditional love and to awaken children's awareness of their innate divinity.

Eric Rogerson is a freelance illustrator and fine artist living in Dana Point, CA. Through his artwork, Eric evokes messages of hope, love, and humanistic truths. His work has been showcased in fine art galleries in San Francisco and New Mexico and in select publications.

STAR CHILD PRESS
A DIVISION OF LIGHT TECHNOLOGY PUBLISHING
PRESENTS

by leia Stinnett

THE LITTLE ANGEL BOOK SERIES

The Little Angel Who Could Not Fly

Meet Angela, the only angel in the Angelic Kingdom who can't fly. As she searches for answers, she learns an important lesson about herself.

$9.95 • Softcover • 64 PP. • 5.5 X 8.5 Perfect Bound • 978-1-62233-025-6

1
Softcover, 8.5 x 11, 91 pp
$18.95 • 978-0-929385-87-7

2
Softcover, 8.5 x 11, 107 PP
$18.95 • 978-0-929385-81-5

3
Softcover, 8.5 x 11, 62 PP
$10.95 • 978-0-929385-80-8

4
Softcover, 5.5 x 8.5, 92 PP
$7.95 • 978-0-929385-96-9

5
Softcover, 5.5 x 8.5, 45 PP
$9.95 • 978-0-929385-64-8

6
Softcover, 5.5 x 8.5, 58 PP
$6.95 • 978-0-929385-90-7

7
Softcover, 5.5 x 8.5, 60 PP
$6.95 • 978-0-929385-88-4

8
Softcover, 5.5 x 8.5, 56 PP
$6.95 • 978-0-929385-91-4

9
Softcover, 5.5 x 8.5, 60 PP
$6.95 • 978-0-929385-84-6

10
Softcover, 5.5 x 8.5, 58 PP
$6.95 • 978-0-929385-83-9

11
Softcover, 5.5 x 8.5, 58 PP
$6.95 • 978-0-929385-86-0

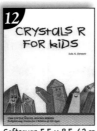

12
Softcover, 5.5 x 8.5, 62 PP
$6.95 • 978-0-929385-92-1

13
Softcover, 5.5 x 8.5, 60 PP
$6.95 • 978-0-929385-89-1

14
Softcover, 5.5 x 8.5, 60 PP
$6.95 • 978-0-929385-85-3

15
Softcover, 5.5 x 8.5, 60 PP
$6.95 • 978-0-929385-82-2

Print books: Visit Our Online Bookstore www.LightTechnology.com
eBooks Available on Amazon, Apple iTunes, Google Play, and Barnes & Noble
Phone: 928-526-1345 or 1-800-450-0985 • Fax: 928-714-1132

STAR CHILD PRESS
A DIVISION OF LIGHT TECHNOLOGY PUBLISHING

PRESENTS

by Lou Bader

The Great Kachina

The Great Kachina
by Lou Bader
illustrated by Mary Toerner

Author Lou Bader weaves two delightful tales of life in northern Arizona. Meet whimsical animal characters, a little girl who can understand them, and a powerful Kachina who could change their lives forever.

$11.95 • Softcover • 64 PP. • Full color • ISBN: 978-0-929385-60-0

by Brian Gold

Cactus Eddie
The Legend of
Written and illustrated by Brian Gold

THE LEGEND OF CACTUS EDDIE

The Legend of Cactus Eddie will bring a smile to your face and tears to your eyes as you follow the adventures of an orphan in the Wild West who is raised by dinosaurs and grows up with the best traits and abilities of the humans and the dinosaurs.

The story is classic Wild West — and combined with the unexpected role that dinosaurs play, it is impossible to put down. Add to a fascinating story Mr. Gold's brilliant art set in the Red Rock Country of Arizona and the result is a must-read for children of all ages.

$11.95 • 60 PP. • 6 x 9 • Softcover • Full color • ISBN: 978-0-929385-74-7

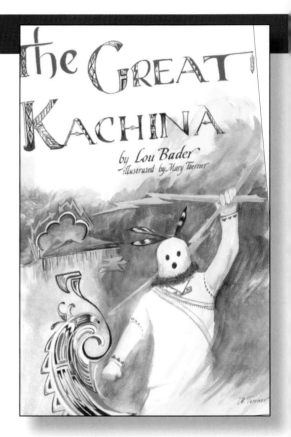